MW00883980

Big-Hearted Charlie Never Gives Up

Fun Adventures

Book 2

ALSO BY KRISTA KEATING-JOSEPH

Big-Hearted Charlie Runs The Mile
Book 1
Royal Palm Literary Award Winner

Big-Hearted Charlie Never Gives Up

Fun Adventures

By Krista Keating-Joseph

Illustrated by Phyllis Holmes

Copyright, 2017
Krista Keating-Joseph

Big-Hearted Charlie Never Gives Up
Fun Adventures

All Rights Reserved

Illustrations by Phyllis Holmes

No text or images in this book
may be used or reproduced in any
manner without written permission
of the copyright holder.

Cover layout and interior pages
layout by Capri Porter.

Printed in the United States of America

ISBN: 978-0-9972523-9-2

Published by
Legacies & Memories
St. Augustine, Florida

(888) 862-2754
www.LegaciesandMemoriesPublishing.com

Contact the Author
Website: www.KristaKeatingJoseph.com
E-mail: kkeatingjoseph@gmail.com

For All the Adventurous Girls and Boys
with the Biggest Hearts,
and to My Big-Hearted Children.

Contents

Dedication

This is a Story About the Adventures of a Boy with the Biggest Heart...

"The newest guy will always teach you something new."

Charlie was so excited to take karate.

"Why do you want to learn karate?" the instructor asked.

Charlie puffed out his chest and said, "I want to be Rambo."

The instructor smiled. "Well, Charlie, you sure want a challenge. You know, what you learn can only be used in the karate studio."

Charlie learned how to do push-ups, sit-ups and kicks.

"Boy, this is a lot harder than it looks," he thought.

"Attitude is everything, kids!" the instructor told the class.

Charlie worked hard. He knew Rambo wouldn't give up, so he wouldn't either. He even practiced karate on his family, even though he wasn't supposed to.

Soon, Charlie felt he was the best Rambo on the block. Then he met Maria!

"Passionate about your job no matter what it is."

Charlie loves visiting Grandma and Grandpa at the beach in Mexico. "Hey, Grandpa, do you still have the Navy SEAL's boat?"

He couldn't wait for the adventures with Grandpa, who let Charlie drive the inflatable boat all by himself. Charlie worked hard to learn to drive it all around the bay.

Once in a while, just for excitement, Grandpa would tip it over to see if Charlie could handle it. And handle it he did! Not only did he show Grandpa he could swim, but he also showed him he could drive the boat to town. Maybe one day, Charlie would even live on a boat!

"Big fish in a small pond."

When Charlie is at the beach in Mexico, there is so much to do. He thought, "Should I drive the inflatable boat, look for shells, build a castle, tease my brother and sister, run down the beach, make a shelter, play box hockey, fly a kite or...."

He notices the neighbor, George, who fishes every day for his food.

"Hey George! May I fish with you?"

"Of course, Charlie, but if you don't catch my dinner, I'll have to eat only rice for supper." George always liked to challenge himself and others.

"You're on, George! If I don't catch a fish for you, I'll eat just rice too!"

At first, Charlie wasn't strong enough to hold the fishing pole. "It seems a lot bigger than a regular fishing pole. Maybe I can't do this," he thought.

George could see Charlie was struggling. "No need to give up," George said. "Here's a smaller pole."

All of a sudden Charlie felt a gigantic tug.

"Pull up hard, then reel it in, C4," George said. C4 was Charlie's nickname.

"I got it! I got it!" Charlie shouted. He struggled, but reeled the fish in and it wiggled onto the sand. Charlie grinned. "George, I guess no rice for dinner!"

"Overcoming Challenges."

"Hey Mom! May I run in the race with you today?" Charlie asked. "You know I'm 7 years old now, so I can keep up with you in the 3-mile race because I am a FAST runner!"

"I know you are a fast runner, but this is FAR," she said. "You can run with me, but let me know when you need to walk and we will walk together."

They ran a slow, steady pace and when they reached a water stop, Charlie thought, "Boy, I really want to stop for some water. I am thirsty and getting tired."

Mom asked, "Do you need to stop?"

"No, I am not going to stop!" Charlie said, as he passed the water station.

Soon, they reached the finish line.

"Wow, Charlie! You never walked. You never gave up."

Charlie felt so proud of his accomplishment.

"Every action affects the bigger picture."

In the summers, Charlie likes to visit Aspen, Colorado. He loves to run and this is a great place to do it.

"Charlie, if you want to be a better runner, you need to work harder," his Mom said.

Charlie decided he would run with the dogs to the top of Aspen Mountain. "This will give me strength to be a better runner if I can make it," he thought.

He packed a small bag with water and snacks and even took a small bowl for the dogs. He was all set to run the trail to the top when his sister Adele caught his eye.

"Charlie, you can't make it to the top of AJAX. It's 12,000 feet."

"I can do it! Just you watch me!" Charlie remembered that Mom had told him he had LOTS of energy and a BIG heart.

As he ran up the trail, he thought "Wow! There are so many slick rocks with mud and I need to watch out for those tree stumps." His foot slipped and down he went into the mud. He was breathing very hard and thought he might not be able to finish the run. But Charlie wasn't going to quit.

A couple of hours later, Charlie reached the top with the biggest smile on his face. He was nearly covered with dirt and mud. Even the dogs were shaking off dirt and adding more to his T-shirt.

"Now the fun begins," Charlie thought. "I get to ride the gondola down the mountain, for FREE!" He looked to his dogs Rocky and Scratchy. "You get to go, too!"

"You'll always be respected if you are passionate."

Charlie loves to body surf in the ocean with his brother.

"Hey, the waves look a little rough today. I think you should stand on the shore until they get smaller," said Charlie.

"I'm not going to get hurt. You just want me to watch you!"

Charlie loves to ride the waves fast with only his body. He tries to be a dolphin in the water.

"Hey Charlie, you OK? That's a lot of sand in your mouth!" his brother yelled as Charlie tumbled over the wave.

Charlie caught his breath and wondered if this was a good idea. He noticed the waves were getting bigger.

"I think I'll catch just one more, just to get the sand out of my swim trunks," he said. He succeeded and made it all the way to the beach without eating sand.

Charlie's next challenge was to surf, but he didn't have a surfboard. At least, not yet.

"(A challenge) brings the best or worst out of you."

One day, Charlie's cousin Bobby asked, "Hey Chuckles, you want to try a surfboard?"

"Are you kidding? Of course, I would!" he replied excitedly. He wanted to learn how to ride the curl of the wave.

Charlie tried and tried to surf. So many times, he flipped over, but he kept trying. He didn't want to leave the water.

After hours in the big waves, Charlie told Bobby, "This is a lot harder than body surfing. I have to push up and then keep my balance!"

After a day of falling, swimming, and paddling, Charlie and his brother finally learned how to surf, but they had very different surfing styles. Charlie would take *every* wave and his brother would spend a lot of time waiting for the perfect one.

"Attention to details."

"OK, Charlie, you are 13. Do you know what that means? SCUBA lessons!" Grandpa shouted.

Everyone knew of the gift Grandpa gave on 13th birthdays and Charlie couldn't wait.

"This is a tough course and you are very young for this," said Charlie's Mom. "You probably won't be able to understand the depth gauges and all the rules. So, don't be disappointed if you have to wait until you're older."

Charlie was never going to let that happen. He studied and practiced in his swimming pool for weeks on end. He was making good progress.

"Mom, as my last test, I have to do one deep dive in the ocean," he said. "I am a little nervous, though."

"You have done everything right and I'm sure you can overcome your nerves. Just stay positive and enjoy the fishy view," she said.

Charlie was worried because he wanted to do everything just right.

Later, he came running into the house, the back door slamming as he entered. "Mom! Mom! I passed! I even saw a Nurse Shark! Luckily, he was sound asleep on the ocean bottom. I wanted to poke him to wake him up, but then I thought that wasn't the best idea!"

"It's already done. Stay proactive."

"Mom, can I ride in a mountain bike race?" Charlie asked.

"I know how much you love to ride your bike, but do you think you can go up desert trails with rocks?" Mom asked, even though she knew that would not stop him from trying. "You know, the hills are not like riding on the street. Mountain bike races here in Arizona are in the desert with sand and snakes!"

"Sounds fun," Charlie said. "I just need a helmet and a mountain bike with gears."

The day of the race was hot and the desert dusty. The start of the race was a lot faster than he had imagined.

As Charlie pushed hard on his pedals on the narrow desert trail, he thought, "I just can't wait to make it to the top of this hill! I know I can make it without falling. YIKES! Watch out for that cactus!"

He struggled as the hill went on and on. "If I stop now, I could never get back on my bike. It is too steep," he thought. Gritting his teeth and clenching his jaw, he made it to the top.

"I did it!"

"Now my favorite part of mountain biking, going downhill!" he said to himself as he let his bike go...."

"No one says that's not my job."

Charlie looks forward to Christmas every year. "Hey guys. I'm the man of the family and I get to pick the tree out this year," he announced, much to the annoyance of his brother and sister.

Mom jumped in and replied, "I have a surprise for you! This year, we are not going to the Christmas tree lot. I have something bigger and better in mind," she said as she showed her children a yellow permit tag.

"The tag is not a tree, Mom," Charlie said with a smirk.

"Of course not, but we are driving to the mountains and we are going to chop down our own tree," she said.

Every child knows that the absolute best thing about chopping a tree down is using an ax.

"Charlie is not strong enough to use that ax. He will chop his hand off," said his sister, Adele.

"I'm sure Charlie will be careful. Look at his big muscles!" Mom said, as Charlie flexed.

After lots of chopping, flying wood chips and blistering, Charlie didn't think he could do it. But he thought, "I can't give up and disappoint my Mom."

He kept chopping and chopping.

Soon, Charlie flashed his Charming-Charlie smile and yelled, "Timberrrr!"

To the delight of his family, they had the perfect Christmas tree and Charlie still had his hand!

"It may be the wrong call, but make it work to your advantage."

Charlie was 14 and saw a young girl on TV flying an airplane.

"Mom, can I learn to fly a plane?"

"I know you are good at math and you made it through your scuba instruction, but do you really think you have the courage to fly a plane?"

"I'll go to flight classes and study every day."

Mom knew he was determined to learn to fly and that his begging would never end. "If you follow the rules and study hard, I'll let you try."

Charlie had very successful flying lessons. He had a *magic touch* with take-offs and landings.

"I am so proud of how you landed that plane," said Mom. "I just have one question. How's the studying going?"

Charlie's smile faded. "I can't seem to get all the work done to get my pilot's license. I'm sorry Mom,"

"I have an idea," said Ron, Charlie's stepfather. "I'll show you how to paraglide and jump off mountains. Ron was a P4 paragliding pilot.

"What?" Charlie yelled. "I'd love to jump off mountains with you!"

Charlie may have failed flying a plane, but he used the information he learned from flight class and take-offs and landings to paraglide with his stepfather by his side.

"I can't believe I get to jump into the sky and float down like a bird without a motor," Charlie said. And, of course, landing with a *magic touch*.

"Staying positive and calming down in a stressful environment."

"Mom! Mom! Mom! I made it!!" Charlie shouted. "They picked me to be on a TV show like survivor for kids. It's called Outward Bound!"

Charlie was so excited. He was only 14 and going to Costa Rica by himself. "I can't wait to river raft, camp out, rock climb, hike and meet new friends for a whole month! I'll be by myself without my brother and sister," he said.

As soon as he arrived, Charlie's group was off into the wilderness, being filmed by many TV cameras. One of their tests was to hike down to the bottom of a cave. It was dark and scary. What they didn't know is that their instructors would turn out all the lights and leave them at the bottom of the cave. The whole group was petrified, until Charlie stepped up.

"OK everyone. I'll lead the way. Grab each other's hands. We'll make a chain and all work together."

The cavern was so dark no one could even *see* their hands. "Hey! Let's all give 150 percent effort. We'll get out of here!" he said.

Charlie's new friends were worried, but he knew he could not give up.

He slowly led the way back to safety through the bats, stalactites and spider webs. When they reached the end of the cave, Charlie looked back at his friends who were all happy to see the light.

"Always have your buddy's back."

Climbing a real rock wall is very different than climbing a wall on the playground. "I can't believe how the ledges are so narrow and the rocks so slippery," Charlie said, "Boy! It's a long way down."

Slowly and carefully, he climbed to the top of the dangerous cliff, where his friend Sloth waited for him. They were in Costa Rica, where there are many cliffs.

Just before Charlie reached the top, he felt his feet slip off the side of the rock ledge. He fell several feet until the rope yanked him back to the wall.

"Sloth, you got me! Whew, thanks!"

"I have my feet back on the ledge. See you in a second," Charlie assured his friend.

"Whoa! I can't believe I made it! It would have been a long way to fall."

He felt exhilarated – and grateful that his buddy had his back.

"Making decisions in a timely manner."

"So, I'm going to run 2 miles – 8 laps while jumping over 3 hurdles and water on every lap?" Charlie questioned his Mom with an expectant smile on his face.

He loved watching others running the Steeplechase because it was unexpected and hilarious when a runner fell into the water.

"I CAN NOT wait to get wet!" Charlie said.

"Charlie, the point is to stay DRY!" Mom reminded him.

"I know Mom. I just love the challenge!"

As he ran the Steeplechase, he started out feeling like a brave warrior, jumping and running with ease. As the laps went by, he realized how difficult it was to finish the race.

"I feel hot and tired. Now, I WANT to fall into the water pit," he thought. But he was determined to complete the race and not get wet.

"Success," Charlie proclaimed as he crossed the finish line where his sister, Adele, was waiting for him with a bucket of water.

"I know what you're going to do with that," he said with his Charming-Charlie smile.

Adele threw the entire bucket of water on him to cool him off from the desert heat.

"Always remember, Jedi, never deal in absolute!"

"So, ladies and gentlemen. What are you planning to do with your future?" Charlie's high school physics teacher and running coach asked his class.

Because Big-Hearted Charlie wasn't shy, his hand shot up first.

"I am going to be a Navy SEAL," he confidently answered.

The teacher grinned and replied, "Charlie, I know you are an amazing runner, but it takes so much more mental and physical stamina to become a Navy SEAL. You need skills, strength, and determination to never give up, even when situations get difficult!"

"Hmmmm, I think I've got this!" Charlie said.

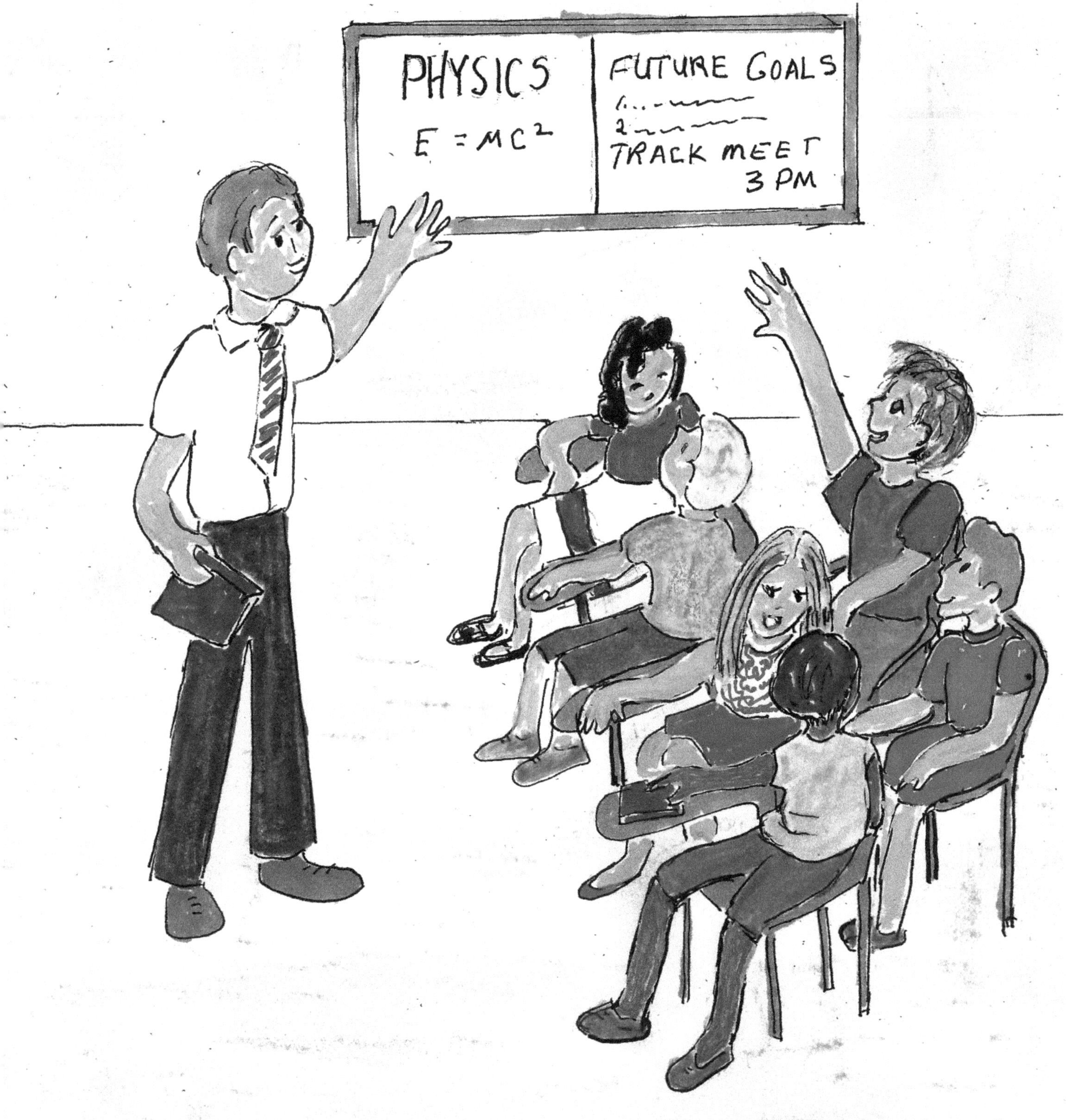
PHYSICS
E = MC2
FUTURE GOALS
1.
2
TRACK MEET
3 PM

"I've been working on my skills my entire life to become a SEAL," Charlie thought with a grin.

Several years later, Charlie was at the school his sister, Ali, attends. When the principal introduced him, Ali proudly announced, "This is my brother, Charlie. He is a Navy SEAL."

The quotations above the stories throughout the book are from Navy SEAL Charles Keating IV during his speech on "Leadership" December 23, 2015 at The Florida Department of Environmental Protection.